# TO THE BEACH

## Thomas Docherty

templar books
an imprint of Candlewick Press

I'm going to the beach.
I've got my goggles and snorkel,

my flippers,

my bucket and shovel,

my bathing suit ...

and my **big** yellow inner tube.

All I need now is . . .

an airplane....

a sailboat . . .

a truck....

a camel . . .

some sand . . .

the sea . . .

and a **friend.**

a helicopter . . .

a bicycle . . .

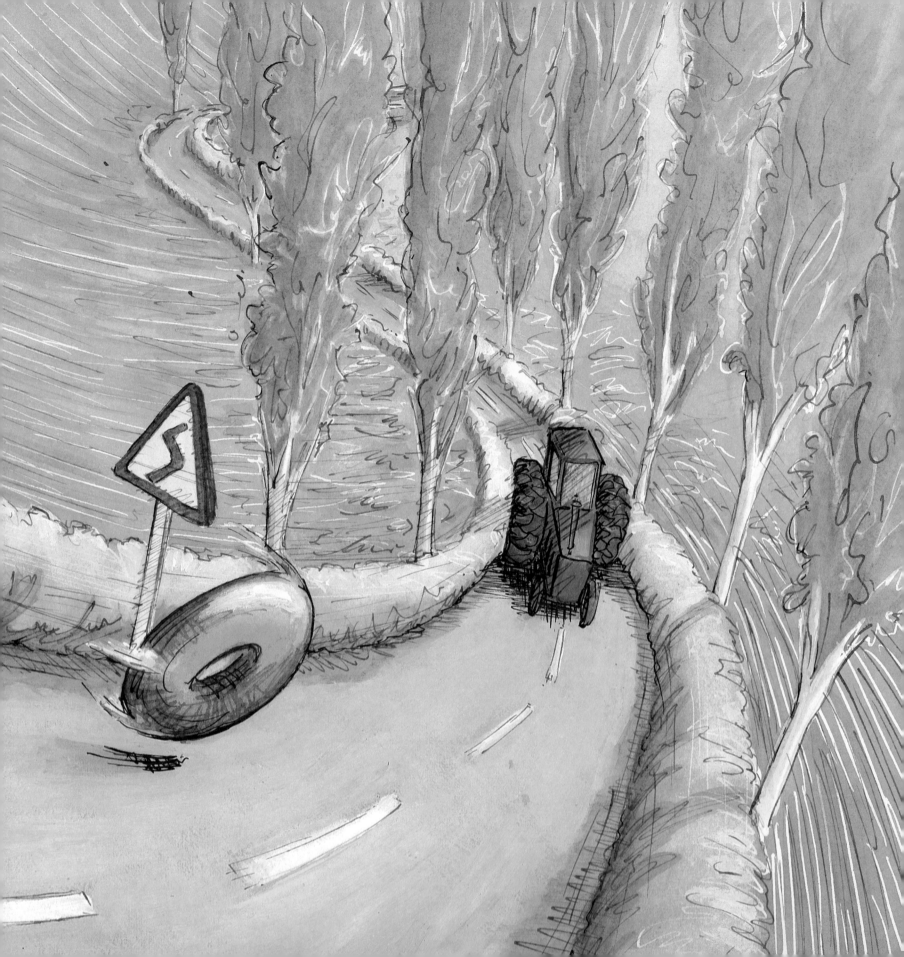

and a tractor.

Home.

So where to next?

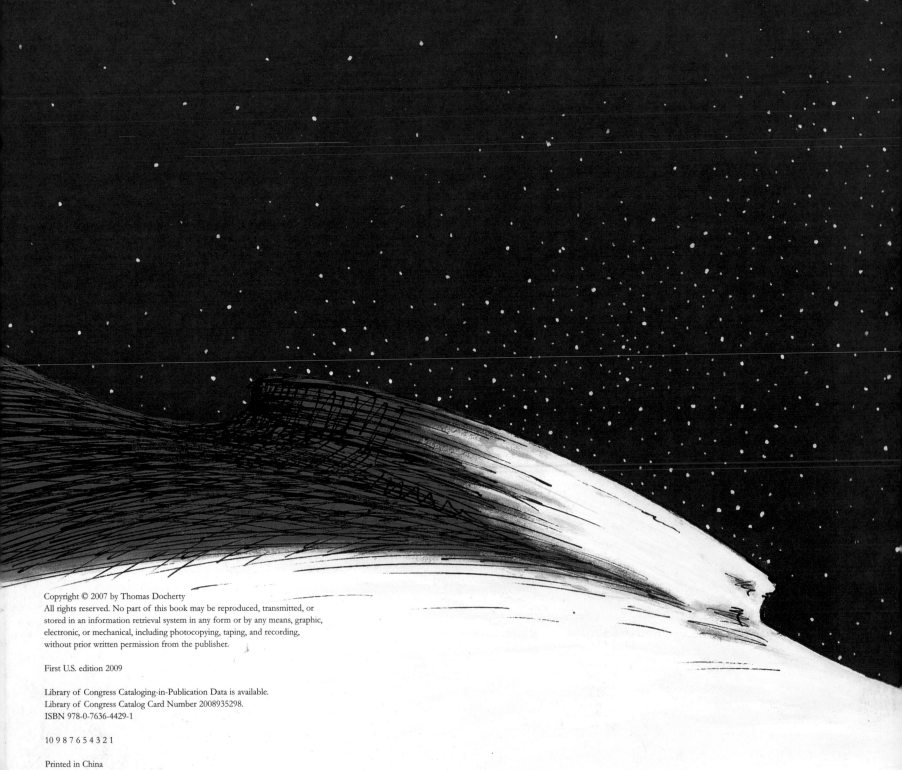

First U.S. edition 2009

Library of Congress Cataloging-in-Publication Data is available.
Library of Congress Catalog Card Number 2008935298.
ISBN 978-0-7636-4429-1

10 9 8 7 6 5 4 3 2 1

Printed in China

This book was typeset in Garamond.
The illustrations were done in watercolor and ink on paper.

A TEMPLAR BOOK

An imprint of
Candlewick Press
99 Dover Street
Somerville, Massachusetts 02144
www.candlewick.com